Sharon
1995
Xmas

The Best-Ever Book of
HORSES

Jackie Budd

Kingfisher

KINGFISHER
An imprint of Larousse plc
Elsley House, 24-30 Great Titchfield Street,
London W1P 7AD

First published by Kingfisher 1995
10 9 8 7 6 5 4 3 2 1

Copyright © Larousse plc 1995

A CIP catalogue record for this book is available from the British Library.

ISBN 1 85697 287 9

Author: Jackie Budd
Series editor: Sue Nicholson
Design: Ben White
   Associates and
   John Jamieson
Cover design:
   John Jamieson
Art editor: Valerie Wright
Picture research: Elaine Willis
Typeset by Tracey McNerney
Printed in Spain

**For Nick, Daniel and Joe,
and Dominic – a 'best-ever' horse**

CONTENTS

ALL ABOUT HORSES

The story of the horse begins way back, at the dawn of time, millions of years before the first people appeared on Earth. It is a story full of adventure and drama which starts with a struggle simply to stay alive.

Running wild

Although there are hardly any true wild horses left today, there are still many horses living in a wild state. Most of these, such as the mustang of North America and the Australian brumby, are actually 'feral' horses that were once domesticated but escaped to live and breed in the wild. The Camargue ponies of southern France roam free but are all owned by people.

▼ **Over millions of years, differences in environment and climate slowly changed the horse. However, since people began to tame, use and breed horses about 3,500 years ago, it has been the human race which has had the greatest influence on the horse story.**

There are still many unanswered questions in our knowledge of how horses evolved. However, by using fossils and other scientific evidence, experts have been able to piece together a fascinating picture of how early horses spread across the world to become the many shapes and sizes of horses we know today.

As the Earth's climate changed, species of animal appeared and disappeared with only the fittest and the most adaptable clinging to existence. By the time people had begun to tame and ride the horse, nature had already created one of the toughest and most talented survivors in the animal kingdom.

Evolution of the horse

Hyracotherium, originally called *Eohippus* or Dawn Horse, was the ancestor of the modern horse. It was only 25 cm tall and had four toes on each foot.

Hyracotherium
(55-40 million years ago)

Mesohippus
(40-25 million years ago)

Mesohippus and *Mery-chippus* were larger than *Eohippus*. They had longer legs and three toes on each foot rather than four.

Gradually, the Earth's dense, wet forests became firm, grassy plains. To avoid extinction, the early horses changed too.

Merychippus
(25-5 million years ago)

Pliohippus
(5-2 million years ago)

Pliohippus had large, flat grinding teeth for feeding on grass and longer, stronger legs supported by hooves.

By the end of the last Ice Age, millions of wild horses that we could recognize roamed Europe and Asia – the species *Equus caballus*.

Equus caballus
(1.5 million years ago)

The horse family

All animals that have a single-toed hoof on the end of each leg belong to the horse family – the genus (group) we call *Equus*. This makes it easy to spot the relatives of the horse, which include zebras, donkeys, asses and mules. But how did horses as unlike each other as the Shetland and the Shire, the Arab and the ass, develop into such different creatures when they shared a common ancestor?

Horse homeland

America was the birth-place of the horse – the only place where fossils of *Eohippus* have been found. Over millions of years, until the last Ice Age separated America from the rest of the world, herds of horses migrated across land bridges to Asia and beyond.

Mighty mustangs

Although the first horses evolved in America, for some reason they became extinct there before the last Ice Age. It was not until Spanish adventurers brought their spirited mounts to the New World that horses returned to the American continent. Some horses escaped or were stolen by Native Americans. These became the ancestors of the mustang (1).

Asses, zebras and donkeys

The earliest and most primitive horses to migrate from America millions of years ago were the ancestors of today's zebras and asses.

The domestic donkey (8) is descended from the African ass.

NORTH AMERICA

SOUTH AMERICA

KEY
1 Mustang
2 Camargue pony
3 Brumby
4 African wild ass
5 Kiang (Tibetan wild ass)
6 Indian onager
7 Common zebra
8 Domestic donkey
9 Przewalski's horse
10 Shire
11 Arab
12 Akhal-Teke
13 Exmoor pony
14 Shetland pony
15 Falabella

Today, there are over 200 breeds of horses and ponies. The smallest is the Falabella (16), which was originally bred in Argentina. It stands just 34 inches (80 cm) tall.

These animals began moving when the climate was still tropical. As it cooled, they wandered south into the Middle East, Asia and Africa. Today there are three races of wild ass – the African (4), the kiang (5) and the onager (6) – and there are three kinds of striped zebra – the common zebra (7), Grevy's zebra and the mountain zebra.

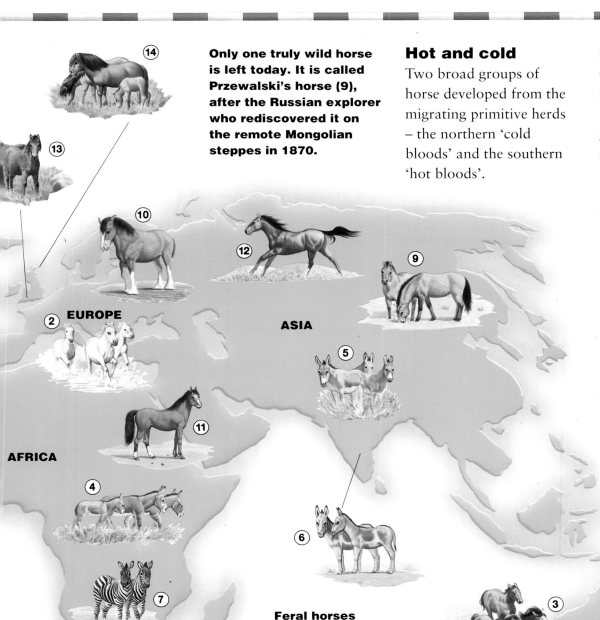

Only one truly wild horse is left today. It is called Przewalski's horse (9), after the Russian explorer who rediscovered it on the remote Mongolian steppes in 1870.

Hot and cold

Two broad groups of horse developed from the migrating primitive herds – the northern 'cold bloods' and the southern 'hot bloods'.

Heavy horses

Cold-blooded horses include the huge Shire (10). The ancestors of this gentle giant migrated into the cool marsh and forest lands of northern Europe after the last Ice Age. With few natural enemies to escape from, these horses grew tall, heavy and slow. Their bulky bodies helped them to survive the cold, and extra bones in the spine gave more room for the digestive organs. Huge feet spread the horse's weight on the soft, muddy ground and hairy 'feathers' kept the legs warm.

EUROPE

ASIA

AFRICA

AUSTRALIA

Feral horses include mustangs (1), Camargue ponies (2) and brumbies (3).

What makes a mule?

Despite being different species, asses and horses can be bred together to create new animals like the mule (from a donkey stallion and horse mare) and the hinny (from a donkey mare and horse stallion). The offspring are very strong and tough, but they are always infertile so they can never produce their own young.

Pony power

A smaller type of horse also spread across Europe and Asia – the pony. It became a specialist at surviving all kinds of harsh climates and conditions. Hardy native British breeds, such as the Exmoor (13) and Shetland (14), grew thick coats and long manes and tails to help them survive the cold.

Fiery horses

The Arab (11), the oldest and purest horse breed, is a hot-blood. Arabs became lean and athletic, with dish-shaped heads adapted to breathing in dry, dusty air and fine hair to cope with the desert heat. Other fast breeds include the Akhal-Teke (12) of Asia.

Danger!

Long before people arrived on the scene, evolution taught horses how to survive. The success of the species depended on avoiding becoming dinner for a passing predator. Therefore, every herd member was constantly on the lookout for danger, ready either to escape as fast as possible or, if necessary, to turn and fight.

▼ On the open African grasslands, young zebras can be an easy catch for a hungry lion.

Fight or flight?

Like any hunted animal, fear is a horse's strongest emotion. When a horse feels threatened, it will panic and react in one of two ways – fight or flight. As it is built for speed, a horse's first instinct is to run from danger. However, if cornered or forced to face an attacker, it is well equipped to kick and bite to defend itself. Bucking is a natural defence reaction, too. That's why young horses may buck when first saddled up.

Horse sense

 Everyone knows at least one rule about being near horses – don't stand behind one or you may get kicked! This isn't because all horses are bad tempered. It's simply easy to forget that despite the fact that they have been domesticated, horses are still wild animals at heart, and almost every horse and pony follows the same basic instincts as the wildest mustang.

Who's boss?

Fighting between horses is quite rare, even in the wild, because living together and keeping the peace is essential to herd life. However, a stallion may fight to ward off a threat from a rival. In a field, horses and ponies have their own 'pecking order' too, with bites and kicks sorting out who's boss.

Making friends with a pony and teaching it to trust you means taking time to learn about and understand what makes it behave the way it does. Ponies are naturally wary and can be easily startled, shying at any sudden, unexpected movement, mainly because attackers often sprang without warning. So always be calm and sensible near a pony, talking and running your hand firmly over its body to let it know where you are.

Grooming

Touch is used between horses to communicate, and they often groom each other by nibbling on one another's necks and backs.

► Horses have their own special body language and facial expressions. If you watch closely, you will soon pick up clues about what a favourite horse or pony is thinking and feeling.

alert

angry

afraid

content

flehmen*

*smelling or tasting something interesting!

Body talk

The overall shape and appearance of a horse or pony is called its conformation. Looking at this shape is one way in which people compare horses. The parts of the horse's body are called the points. Learning to recognize these points is useful as you will hear them talked about at your riding school or by a farrier or vet.

What makes a good horse?

Look at the ponies in a nearby field or at your riding school. Few have a perfect conformation. Some features of 'poor' conformation are to do with being unattractive or out of proportion, such as having a too-large head. Others can indicate a physical weakness and are more serious.

Muscle-bound

This amazing drawing of a horse's muscles is from *The Anatomy of the Horse* by George Stubbs (1724–1806). Stubbs was the first artist to study a horse's body in detail. As a result, his drawings and paintings were very realistic.

Poll   Crest   Mane   Neck   With

Forelock   Eye   Nostril   Cheek

Ears   Muzzle   Shoulder   Knee   Chest   Cannon bone   Belly   Stifle   Hoof   Elb   Forearm

Hands high

Horses are measured from the ground to the withers and their height is given in 'hands' – a measurement of 10.2 cm (or 4 inches), which is actually based on the width of a man's hand. The exceptions are Shetland ponies and miniature horses which are measured in inches.

◄ A small horse 14.2 hh (hands high) or less is termed a pony.

Skeleton

A horse's skeleton gives clues about its breed. For example, a carthorse will have thick, heavy bones to support its weight whereas a racehorse will have long, fine bones.

Back
Loins
Croup
Dock
Tail
Quarters
Flank
Thigh
Hock
Fetlock
Coronet
Pastern

Bony framework

At first glance, a horse's skeleton looks very different to ours, but take a closer look. There are more similarities than you would think!

HUMAN	HORSE
1 finger- & toenail	1 hoof
2 wrist	2 knee
3 elbow	3 elbow
4 heel	4 hock
5 knee	5 stifle

Horses and ponies come in all shapes and sizes. Although each breed has its own characteristics, all horses are built in much the same way. Even after thousands of years of living with people, horses are still designed to gallop fast to escape predators and have the stamina to keep up with a moving herd.

Walk

The paces

Paces, or gaits, describe the way a horse moves. By using different gaits, a horse can increase or decrease its speed and still remain in balance. We have two gaits – walking and running. With only two legs, the sequence of our footfalls remains the same but is quickened. Having twice as many legs as we do, it's not surprising that horses have more gaits.

④

The jump

Although horses rarely need to leap obstacles in the wild, jumping comes naturally because the action is just like an extra-big canter stride.

The walk

This is the slowest pace, where you can clearly hear the hoofbeats come down in an even 'one-two-three-four' sequence. The horse starts with one hindleg, then the foreleg on the same side, then the opposite hindleg, then that foreleg. There are always at least two feet on the ground at any time.

The trot

This is a horse's most natural pace where it springs from one diagonal pair of legs to the other, with a moment in between when all four legs are off the ground. **③**

A true jump has five stages:
(1) Approach – the horse steadies and dips its head to get the jump in focus.
(2) Take-off – it brings its quarters underneath and lifts its shoulders and forelegs.

Gallop

Trot

The canter

In the canter, there are three distinct beats. First one hindfoot, then the other hindfoot with its opposite forefoot, then the other forefoot striking out on its own (the 'leading leg') and finally a moment of silence when all four feet are off the ground.

The gallop

This is the fastest and most exciting pace. The gallop is basically a canter with extra speed and longer strides. When it is galloping, the horse's hindlegs push it forwards with greater power. Racehorses can gallop at speeds of up to 72 km/h!

There are four gaits which come naturally to the horse – the walk, trot, canter and gallop – and each gait has its own particular pattern of hoofbeats. Some horses also have specialized gaits which they have either been trained to do or which are in their breeding.

(3) Flight – the horse rounds its back and stretches out to clear the fence.
(4) Landing – the forelegs straighten out, then touch down.

As the hind legs land, the horse lifts its front end, then strides away.

Canter

Colours and markings

Wall eye

There are so many different colours and markings that every horse and pony you see is quite unique. This is helpful when it comes to recognizing or describing a particular one. But why are there so many colours? For the answer, we have to go back in time again, to look at the horse's ancestors.

Blaze

▲ Horses usually have deep brown eyes but you may sometimes see a wall eye – a white or white-blue eye.

Sock

Pastern

14

▼► White hairs often come in small patches on the head and the lower legs. A horse or pony with no markings is known as whole-coloured.

White face

Stripe

Star

Snip

Coronet

Stocking

▲ Leg markings are often described according to the area they cover, such as a white heel, or white fetlock.

⑪

Mix and match

What makes a chestnut, a bay or a dapple grey? It's all to do with the colour of the coat's individual hairs. Each hair either has a pigment (colouring) or it does not. Hairs without pigment are white. Those with pigment are red or black. The mixture of white, red and black in the coat, and the shade of the red hairs, give us all the horse colours we can see.

KEY
1 **Chestnut** – mixture of red and black
2 **Appaloosa** – dark spots on white coat
3 **Fleabitten grey** – flecks of black or brown on white
4 **Palomino** – pale chestnut with white mane and tail
5 **Black** – all black
6 **Dun** – sandy brown with black mane and tail
7 **Piebald** – large irregular black-and-white patches
8 **Bay** – reddish brown with black mane and tail
9 **Dapple grey** – mottle effect of white and black
10 **Brown** – dark red and black
11 **Strawberry roan** – white hairs sprinkled through chestnut

Over the ages, horses' coats became camouflaged so that they blended in with their surroundings – whether it was sand, rock, scrub or a grassy plain – and the rest of the herd. The harder it was for their enemies to see them, especially at the dangerous hours of dusk, the greater their chance of survival.

Painted ponies
People have always prized certain distinctive coat colours. For example, Native Americans liked 'coloured' horses with dramatic piebald or skewbald markings. When they rode into battle, they often painted their ponies with special marks, too, to bring good luck.

▼ This painting by Amos Bad Heart Bull, an Oglala Sioux from Pine Ridge Reservation, shows Crazy Horse and Sitting Bull mounted before warriors at the battle of the Little Bighorn in 1876.

1 Neat yard

Look for a tidy yard and tack room, with clean, roomy stables kept in good repair.

2 Happy horses

Make sure ponies look content, well-fed and alert. Check that their feet are in good condition and they have no sore spots.

3 Muck heap

The muck heap should be neat and tucked away from the stables, and should be cleaned regularly.

5 Safety first

Tools must be put away carefully and First Aid and fire equipment must be close at hand. No smoking is a strict rule in stable yards.

4 Friendly welcome

A well-run school will have polite and cheerful staff who will be happy to help you.

GOING RIDING

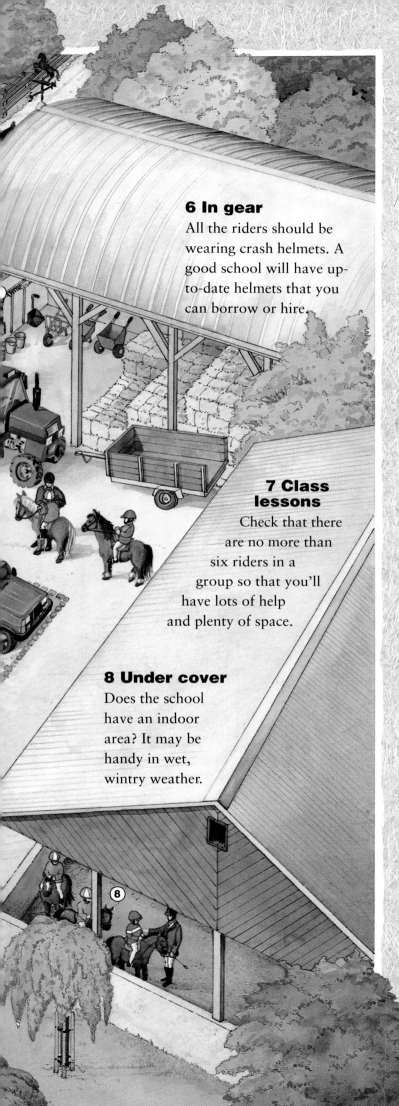

6 In gear

All the riders should be wearing crash helmets. A good school will have up-to-date helmets that you can borrow or hire.

7 Class lessons

Check that there are no more than six riders in a group so that you'll have lots of help and plenty of space.

8 Under cover

Does the school have an indoor area? It may be handy in wet, wintry weather.

A riding school is where most people first meet horses and ponies close-up. Schools can be large, busy yards or small places with only a few ponies. Whatever the size, it is important to choose a good riding school so that you can learn to ride properly. A well-run yard will have horses suitable for beginners and qualified instructors to make riding safe and fun.

Lunge line

This young rider is having a lesson on the lunge. The instructor controls the pony using a long rein called the lungeing rein. This means the rider can concentrate on her position and balance. These lessons are a good way of building up a beginner's confidence.

Ask local horse experts, such as a farrier, a saddler or a Pony Club secretary, which riding school they can recommend. Schools approved by recognized riding organizations will guarantee high standards. Once you have found the right one, book up a lesson – happy riding!

1 Casual kit

For casual riding you can wear a jockey-skull type of crash helmet. The one here is shown with a silk peaked cover. Choose a loose-fitting top with long sleeves even if it is sunny. Wrap up warm in cold weather and wear a waterproof when it's wet.

2 Gymkhana

If you take part in a gymkhana or a small show, you'll need a skull cap with a dark velvet cover, a white or pale shirt with a club tie or plain dark one, a tweed or 'hacking' jacket, and light coloured jodhpurs.

The riding kit

When you're riding, you must wear gear that is safe, comfortable and practical. If you go to a show or to another smart event, you have to get kitted out correctly. However, when you first start riding, it's not essential to have lots of expensive clothing. What's most important is that you have sensible footwear with a small heel, and a well-fitting riding hat that is up to the latest approved standards.

Gloves

Frozen hands won't work well and sweaty ones slip on the reins so always wear gloves – woolly ones in winter, thin cotton ones in summer and leather ones at shows.

Boots

Short jodhpur boots with a low heel are ideal for young riders. Long boots can be leather or rubber, but must fit closely to your legs.

Jodhpurs

Jodhpurs are the most comfortable leg gear, although thick, loose trousers or jeans will do at first. Jodhpurs are made of stretchy fabric with knee panels to prevent saddle rubs.

④ Skull cap

dy otector

3 At a show

Appearing at a larger show means a slightly different look. Wear a skull cap with a dark velvet cover or a hard hat with a fixed peak. Most riders wear either a black or a navy jacket, jodhpurs or breeches – short 'jods' which end just below the knee – and long boots.

4 Cross-country

Safety comes first when riding cross-country. Hats must be top-quality skull caps. A body protector is also essential. Its padded jacket fits under or over a jumper and it may have shoulder pieces.

Air space

Padding

Lining

Chin strap

Choosing a hat*

Your hard hat or crash helmet must:

- have thick, all-over inside padding
- be snug, but not tight, and sit level
- allow two fingers underneath at the back

- cover your temples, forehead and the back of your head
- stay in place when you bend over, even when unfastened.

When wearing your hat, remember to always do the chin strap up tightly.

In the past, riding gear was not as safe and sensible as it is today. Imagine galloping over fields and hedges dressed up like the 18th-century lady shown on the right! In the 1700s and 1800s, most wealthy ladies rode side-saddle – they perched with one leg looped over the hook of a special saddle, which was designed so that both legs rested on the same side of the horse. They sometimes wore a hat with a veil and a long heavy skirt, or habit.

Sitting pretty

Today, some brave lady riders keep the side-saddle tradition alive, and side-saddle classes are still popular at shows.

▶ Riding kit from the late 1700s.

*In Britain, look for the BSI kitemark label to check that a hat has been safety tested. BS 4472 or 6473 are the numbers to watch out for.

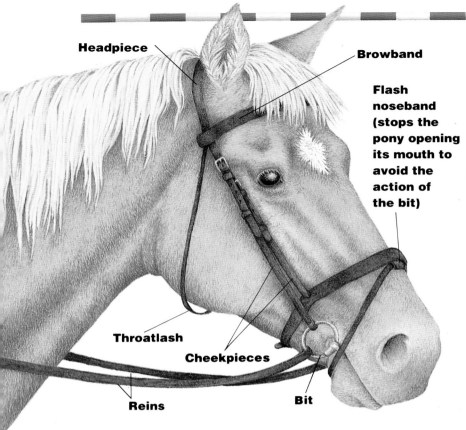

Headpiece

Browband

Flash noseband (stops the pony opening its mouth to avoid the action of the bit)

Throatlash

Cheekpieces

Reins

Bit

Bridles and bits

Tack, or saddlery, is the name given to all the equipment a horse or pony wears when it is ridden. There are many different pieces of tack and each piece has a special use, but the two main items that every pony wears are a saddle and a bridle. Both are usually made of leather and must fit well to be comfortable and effective.

The bridle is basically a set of straps that fasten around the pony's head and support the bit in its mouth. The reins attached to the bit are your communication lines to the pony.

Bits and pieces

There are many kinds of bit and each type works in a slightly different way. Most quiet ponies wear a simple snaffle bit. Stronger ponies may need a curb bit with a curb chain, such as a Pelham. A double bridle is used by skilled riders and well-trained horses for very finely-tuned control.

▲ **Snaffle** – a straight bar, or with a single or double joint in the centre.

▲ **Pelham** – usually has two reins but may have one if a rounding is used.

Curb chain

▲ **Double** – has two bits, a thin bridoon (snaffle) and a curb (such as this Weymouth). Each bit has its own rein and only one rein is used at a time.

Pelham bridle

Double bridle

Cavesson noseband

Rounding

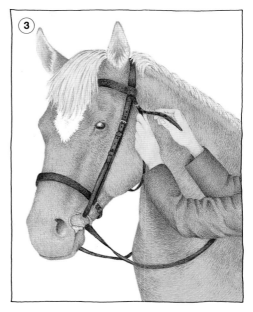

Putting on a bridle

1 Facing forwards, stand close to the pony's near (left) side and put the reins over its head. Hold the bridle so the bit is in front of the mouth and guide in the bit with your left hand. You may need to slip your thumb into the side of the gums where there are no teeth to encourage the pony to open up its mouth.

2 Gently bring the headpiece up over the ears, one by one. Then pull out the forelock and tidy the mane. Check that the bit is at a comfortable height. It should just wrinkle the pony's lips so that it looks like it's smiling. Make sure that the bit is not too high and tight or too low and droopy. Use the bridle's cheekpieces to adjust the height of the bit.

3 Buckle the throatlash, making sure that four fingers will easily fit between the strap and the pony's cheek. Check that the noseband is lying under the cheekpieces. It should sit level, midway between the pony's cheekbone and the bit. Fasten the noseband snugly but leave room for two fingers to fit underneath. Make sure the straps are securely in their keepers.

The bit sits over the pony's tongue in the space between the front and back teeth. Most bits are made of stainless steel, although the mouthpiece may be made of rubber or plastic. The reins are attached to the rings on each side of the mouthpiece, which also stop the bit from sliding through the mouth.

Martingale

Martingales

You may see a horse or pony wearing a neckstrap which has other straps running to the bridle or reins and to the girth. This is called a martingale. It is used to stop the horse throwing up its head so high that riding it is difficult. The running martingale pictured on the left divides into two straps through which each rein is threaded. A standing martingale has one strap which fastens directly to a plain cavesson noseband.

Saddles and stirrups

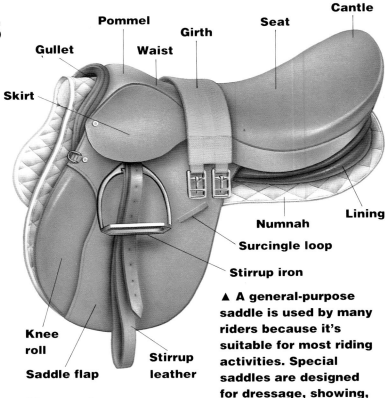

Pommel

Cantle

Gullet

Waist

Girth

Seat

Skirt

Numnah

Lining

Surcingle loop

Stirrup iron

Knee roll

Saddle flap

Stirrup leather

The saddle keeps you sitting securely on the pony's back in the correct position so that you can give the pony aids, or signals, with your legs in the right place on its sides. It is essential that the saddle – and all tack – fits properly to make sure that it isn't causing the horse any discomfort. A saddler is usually the best person to check this.

▲ A general-purpose saddle is used by many riders because it's suitable for most riding activities. Special saddles are designed for dressage, showing, jumping, endurance riding and racing.

Numnah
The numnah is a cotton, sheepskin or rubber pad which is put on under the saddle for extra comfort.

Putting on a saddle
1 Hold the saddle with your left hand on the pommel and your right hand under the seat. Standing on the near side, place the saddle gently on the highest part of the withers then slide it down to the correct position.

2 Let down the girth then take the girth from under the horse's belly and buckle it up beneath the saddle flaps.

3 Pull down the buckle guard. Run down (lower) the stirrups when you are ready to ride.

▶ Protective boots guard against bumps and cuts either from the pony's other legs or if it knocks a jump.

Patterns carved into the leather for grip

High pommel, or horn, for tying on the lasso

Fender

Girth, or 'cinch'

Snaffle bit with long cheeks, or 'shanks'

Western tack

Western riding was developed by the US cavalry and cowboys from classic Spanish riding techniques. The Western saddle was designed for a horse and rider spending hours or days on the range. Its deep seat spread the weight of the rider and kept him secure, and wide leather flaps called fenders became part of the stirrup leathers to protect the legs.

Every saddle is built around a wooden or plastic frame called a tree. Its cushioned panels help to place your weight evenly, making it easier for the pony to carry you. The stirrups aren't attached to the saddle but hang from bars under the skirt. A girth made of leather, cotton or webbing fits around the pony's belly to hold everything in place.

Cleaning tack

Leather needs regular care to keep it supple and safe to use. Ideally, tack should be cleaned after each ride. Once a week it must be taken apart and all the pieces cleaned thoroughly. Here's how to do a quick clean:

1 Wash the bit and wipe the stirrup irons with a clean damp cloth.

2 Hang the bridle on a high hook and put the saddle on a saddle horse or over your knee.

3 Wipe the leatherwork on both sides with a damp cloth

but don't get the leather too wet.

4 Dampen the soap and rub the sponge into it, taking care not to make too much lather. Soap the leather with the sponge then polish it with a soft dry cloth.

High hook for bridle

23

Lifestyles

Given a choice, most ponies would certainly prefer to live outdoors rather than in a stable. Being outside is closest to a horse's natural way of life. However, although being at grass may be a natural kind of lifestyle, there's much more to the outdoor life than simply letting a pony loose in the nearest field. Great care must be taken to choose a field that is both safe and suitable.

▼ Keep pasture in good condition by resting it occasionally and picking up droppings regularly.

Gate
Make sure the gate is wide, sturdy and pony-proof. Care must be taken whenever leading a pony

Fencing
Horses are amazingly accident-prone and great escape artists! Fences must be secure, safe and kept in good repair. Thick hedges or post and rail are best. Any wire needs to be kept taut.

Shelter
A pony in a field cannot move to find shelter like its wild cousins can. Trees offer some protection from bad weather or hot summer sun, but ideally you should provide a purpose-built shelter.

Poisonous plants

Tasty grazing contains herbs and grasses which are good for horses – but watch out for poisonous plants. Here are some common ones:

1 Henbane
2 Ragwort
3 Hemlock
4 Ground ivy
5 Foxglove
6 Horsetail
7 Buttercup
8 Laurel
9 Oak
10 Privet
11 Yew
12 Laburnum

► **Horses and ponies kept in a stable rely on us for their every need.**

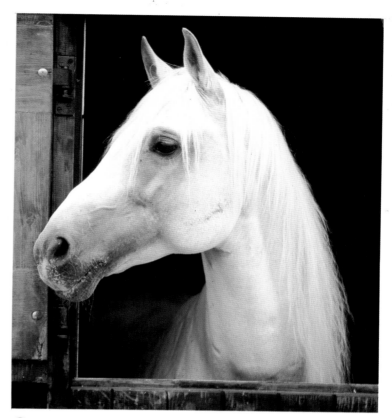

Stable life

Horses weren't designed to live indoors but many are kept that way because it's often easier for us to look after them. Ideally, every horse should go out into a field for a while each day.

Good grass

The amount of goodness in grass can vary. Pasture needs to be well-drained and neither too rich nor too sour. There should be at least 6,000 sq m (1½ acres) of grass per pony.

Some ponies are better suited to living outdoors than others. Hardy breeds will grow thick winter coats to cope with all weathers. Finer-bred types with Arab or Thoroughbred ancestry will need the help of a rug and extra food to keep warm in cold conditions.

Water

Every field needs a constant supply of fresh water, either piped to a trough or from a clean, free-flowing stream.

Company

Lonely ponies are unhappy ponies. Always provide a field-mate such as a donkey or, preferably, another horse.

▲ **Field-kept ponies should be visited twice a day to check that they are all right.**

In the past, horses were often tied up in stalls which meant that many could be kept in a small area. Today, however, most horses and ponies have the freedom of a loose box, built of timber, stone or brick. In the United States, stabling is often built inside the shelter of a large barn. Deep beds of straw or woodshavings keep stabled horses warm and comfortable but they must be kept very clean.

Yard routine

Horses love routine. A stabled pony will soon get to know when to expect a visit, so it is unkind and even harmful to change the times you arrive each day.

Daily tasks

Some jobs, such as tidying up the muck heap or disinfecting the floor of the loose box, can be done once a week but others need doing every day:

1 **Cleaning tack**
2 **Filling water buckets**
3 **Feeding – you should provide at least two feeds a day, morning and evening, with lunch for hard-working ponies**
4 **Filling haynets**
5 **Mucking out and tidying the yard**
6 **Grooming**
7 **Generally checking the horses and adjusting rugs**
8 **Turning out the pony if it's going into a field, or exercising it – a stabled pony needs riding for at least 1¹/₂ hours a day)**

Hay store

Tack room

Feed bins

Loose box

Deep bed

▼ **If you own a pony, find a daily stable routine that fits in with school and stick to it.**

The ideal stable

The minimum size for a loose box or an individual stable is 4.3 m x 3.6 m for a horse and 3.6 m x 3 m for a pony. The box should be 3 m high and the door 1.25 m high and 2.2 m wide. It should have good ventilation, a non-slip floor sloping slightly for drainage, and two tie rings, one on each side, about 1.5 m high.

▶ **Stable-kept horses and ponies need exercising every day.**

In the stable

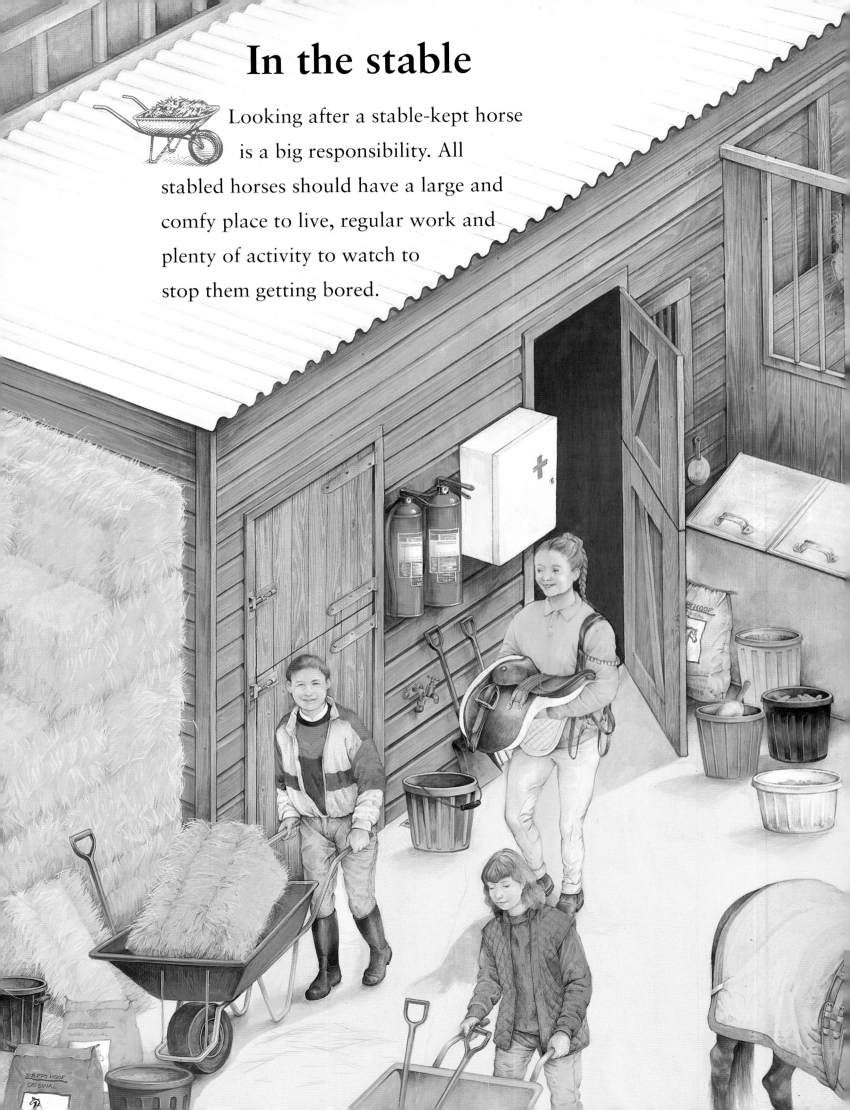

Looking after a stable-kept horse is a big responsibility. All stabled horses should have a large and comfy place to live, regular work and plenty of activity to watch to stop them getting bored.

Grooming

Grooming means more than just brushing all the muddy bits off a pony to make it look smart. Regular grooming cleans the pony's skin and keeps it really healthy. If plenty of hard work is put into brushing, it will even help the blood circulation and improve the pony's muscle tone. What better way to get to know a pony than to give it a relaxing wash and brush up.

Grooming kit

1 Rubber curry comb
2 Metal curry comb
3 Plastic curry comb
Curry combs are used to help clean the body brush; also for removing caked-on dirt and mud or loose hairs. The metal curry comb must never be used on the pony.
4 Body brush
Soft brush with close-packed hairs used to clean the coat and skin deep down.
5 Dandy brush
Stiffer brush with long bristles; too hard for use on the head, mane or tail.
6 Water brush
Similar to the dandy brush but with softer, shorter bristles. Used dampened to smooth the mane or scrub the hooves.
7 Hoof oil and brush
Brushed on to the whole foot when dry to keep the hooves in good condition.
8 Mane comb
For combing out

knots or burrs in the mane and tail.
9 Sponges
For freshening up the pony's eyes, mouth, nostrils and dock.
10 Sweat scraper
For wiping off excess water. Use the hard edge on the body and the flexible edge on the legs.
11 Stable rubber
Soft cloth for polishing the coat or drying wet areas.
12 Hoof pick
For removing bedding, caked mud and stones from the hooves.

Quick-release knot

A special safety knot must always be used for tying up ponies. This quick-release knot can be undone in a blink in an emergency. It should always be tied to a loop of string attached to a tie ring or fence, never directly to the ring or fence itself.

1 Make a loop in the leadrope and put it through the string. Twist the loop several times.

2 Loop the free end of the rope and push it through the twisted loop.

3 To tighten, pull on the end of the rope attached to the headcollar.

Twist

① ② ③

Free end

Pull this end to release

Pull this end to tighten.

◄ Warm New Zealand rugs are used for ponies kept outside.

Rugs

A stabled pony can't move around much to keep warm so it needs at least one stable rug with extra layers on hand if it has been clipped. Modern stable rugs are usually made of quilted synthetic fabric, rather like a duvet, and fasten under the belly.

① ② ③ ④

Clipping

During the colder months of the year, horses and ponies grow thick coats and may get too hot if they are ridden regularly and if they mostly live indoors. That's why they are clipped. How much of the coat is clipped off depends on what kind of work the pony has to do and how much time it spends out at grass. Most ponies don't mind being clipped but it is a skilled job.

KEY
1 Full clip 2 Hunter clip
3 Blanket clip 4 Trace clip

Plaiting

After clipping and grooming, a pony's mane and tail can be plaited, especially if it's going to a show.

▼ Use each tool in the hand nearest the pony's head. So when grooming its near (left) side use your left hand and on its off (right) side use your right hand.

Brushing tips

● Always brush in the direction the coat lies.
● Start near the head then work along the body and down the legs.
● Use firm strokes, putting the weight of your body behind each stroke.
● Only groom when the coat is dry.
● Pick off awkward lumps of mud with your fingers.
● Fasten the head collar around the neck before grooming the head so you groom it properly.
● In cold weather leave at least one rug or blanket on when grooming to keep off the chills. Fold it back in sections as you groom.
● Most ponies love being groomed but some have ticklish areas. Watch out for fidgeting or flicking ears that may tell you a nip or even a kick may be on the way.
● Don't forget to clean the grooming kit too!

Ponies living outside all or most of the time need their coats to be as waterproof as posssible. These ponies only need a light groom, otherwise you will remove the natural grease that keeps them warm and dry. Stable-kept ponies can be given a thorough grooming every day to add a real sparkle to their coats.

Strapping a horse

This is a full grooming given to a stabled horse. Professional grooms finish off by wisping – thumping the muscles using a pad made of twisted hay or straw to get the circulation going and massage and harden the horse's muscles.

Using a hoof pick

A pony's feet need to be cleaned out twice a day to dislodge mud and stones or dirty stable bedding. The foot should be held by its front part and cleaned from heel to toe. This avoids hurting the sensitive frog (the 'V'-shaped part of the sole).

▲ The hoof pick is an essential part of the grooming kit.

An individual diet

What a particular pony needs to eat depends on its size (big horses eat more than little ponies), how much it is exercised, whether it is kept in a stable or out at grass, and its age (young and old ponies have different needs). Feed more in cold weather when a lot of energy is used up keeping warm.

Food and feeding

As every horse and pony is different, each one must be given a diet which caters for its particular needs. However, whether a pony is large or small, fit or fat, its menu must be based on special feeding rules. Every horse or pony needs its diet to provide it with carbohydrates for energy and warmth, protein to build and repair its body, fats for heat and energy, fibre to help digestion, and vitamins and minerals for general good health.

◀ **Meals can be given in a manger (a trough in a stable) or simply in a bucket.**

KEY
1 Flaked maize – for energy and to help a pony put on weight
2 Pony nuts – balanced mixture of food pressed into cubes or pellets
3 Bran – for extra fibre

4 Coarse mix – ready-made mixture, as nuts
5 Chaff – chopped straw with added molasses, for fibre

▲ To find out a horse's or pony's weight, it can be taken to a weighbridge or measured around the girth with a special measuring tape.

6 Dried sugar beet – good source of fibre; must be soaked
7 Salt block – to replace minerals
8 Rolled oats – for horses doing lots of work
9 Flaked barley – for energy and condition

⑥

⑦

⑨

⑧

Feeding facts

A pony needs to eat roughly 2% of its bodyweight in food every day. An average 14 hh pony weighs around 350 kg, so it'll eat about 7 kg of food a day. The less the pony is ridden, the more of this can be given as bulk feed (such as grass and hay) and less as concentrates (such as pony nuts).

During the warmer months, grass is all that most ponies need to eat. However, when grass is poor or unavailable, they should be fed on hay. Hay is simply grass that has been cut and dried when it is at its best. Grass and hay are called bulk feeds. Although they are the main sources of fibre which keep the pony's digestive system working properly, they don't contain much energy. Therefore ponies should be fed other foods, such as pony nuts and cereals, whenever extra energy is needed. These foods are called concentrates, or hard feeds.

Golden rules of feeding
- Feed little and often.
- Always provide plenty of fresh water – a horse can drink up to 55 litres a day.
- Allow an hour or more after feeding before you ride.
- Keep to a set routine.
- Make no sudden changes in diet.
- Feed plenty of fibre, such as hay or chaff.
- Feed lots of succulents, such as carrots and apples.
- Give only the best-quality foods.
- Keep buckets and scoops clean.

Fit and healthy

 Two important people help to keep a well-cared-for horse or pony in the best of health – the vet and the farrier.

Getting to know the signs when a pony is feeling off-colour helps its owner decide when to call the vet. Illness or injury aren't the only times a visit may be needed. A vet helps with routine health care, too, such as rasping (filing down) the teeth, injections and worming.

Common illnesses

Ponies can easily get laminitis, a painful crippling disease often caused by over-feeding. Another common illness is colic, a kind of horsey stomachache usually a result of feeding mistakes. Colic should be suspected if a pony is off its food, restless and sweaty with a high temperature (normal is 38°C), and the vet should be called immediately.

▶ **Horses need yearly vaccinations to help stop them catching two very dangerous diseases – tetanus and equine 'flu. The vet can give both injections in one go.**

Warning: Worms

All horses and ponies carry worm parasites inside them. A pony will eat worm eggs along with grass. As the worm larvae grow, they cause the pony to lose weight or get stomachache. Dosing a horse or pony every 6-8 weeks with worming powder or paste helps to keep worms at bay.

Lameness

Horses can go lame due to an injury or an illness. A wound, heat or swelling usually shows the vet the cause.

▲ **If a horse goes lame, trotting up will show which leg is causing the problem, and often why. The horse is led away from the vet and back again at a walk and trot.**

Health checklist

Watching a pony carefully will soon show whether or not it is feeling well. It should have:
- ears pricking to and fro, so that it looks alert
- glossy coat lying flat
- loose and supple skin
- a good appetite
- a good thirst
- regular bowel movements
- bright eyes
- no puffiness or heat in the legs
- body filled out with good muscle tone, but not fat
- weight distributed evenly on all four feet.

Hoof care

A pony needs to see the farrier every 4-6 weeks to trim back hoof growth (the horn) and replace any worn shoes with new ones.

A horse's hooves are growing all the time, just like our fingernails. Because wild horses and ponies are always on the move over rough land, their hardy feet wear naturally into shape. Ponies living in a stable or a small field would soon grow uncomfortably long hooves, which may crack if not trimmed.

When a pony is ridden often, its hooves wear down faster than they can grow. That's why most horses and ponies wear metal shoes, especially if they are ridden on hard surfaces.

Wall of hoof

Toe

▼ This fullered shoe is used for most riding horses and ponies. It is grooved to lighten its weight and give extra grip.

Bulb of heel

Cleft of frog

Bar

Shoe

Sole   **Point of frog**

▼ The farrier heats a steel shoe in a furnace, tries it against the pony's foot for size, then hammers it into shape for a perfect fit before nailing it on. Farriers are so skilled that shoeing doesn't hurt the pony at all.

IN THE PAST

 Long ago, by the light of flickering torches, prehistoric people drew pictures of running horses on the walls of their caves. The people were hunters, and the horses their prey.

However, as time passed, this particular source of food became

▲ Statue of an Etruscan archer, *circa* 500 BC.

instead a useful beast of burden, a precious possession and a symbol of folklore and legend. Through the centuries, the horse has become our workmate, friend and partner, and has come to share with us a very special bond.

▲ Knight from the Isle of Lewis chess set, mid- to late-1100s.

▶ Indian miniature painting of the Mogul emperor Shah Jahan out riding with one of his sons, 1615.

◀ Cave painting at Lascaux, France, around 15,000 BC.

39

Myth and magic

When Stone Age people painted horses on the walls of caves, they may have been conjuring up spirits to help them with the hunt. Since then, horses have often been used in religious rituals and even worshipped.

The first tribespeople to master the art of taming and riding the horse gained speed and power beyond their wildest dreams. It's no wonder that in people's imagination horses took on magical powers, and became part of legend and folklore across the world.

▼ **Bellerophon riding Pegasus**

◄ **Most centaurs were warlike and loved to fight.**

Centaurs

The centaur of Greek mythology had the head and shoulders of a man with the lower body and legs of a horse. Centaurs were passionate and warlike and liked to drink. The most famous centaur was called Chiron. Unlike most of the others, he was wise and just. Chiron taught hunting, medicine and music to Achilles and other famous Greek heroes. Legend says that when Chiron was killed by Hercules, Zeus, the father of the gods, honoured him by placing him among the stars as the constellation Centaurus, along with another centaur, Sagittarius.

Pegasus

Pegasus was a beautiful white winged stallion. A Greek legend tells how Bellerophon tamed Pegasus with the help of the goddess Athene, and how Pegasus helped him defeat a fire-breathing monster. But when Bellerophon tried to fly Pegasus to Mount Olympus, the home of the gods, Zeus sent a gadfly to sting the horse. Pegasus bucked and threw Bellerophon to Earth, flying on to Mount Olympus alone.

Odin and Sleipnir

Odin was the king and father of all the gods of Viking mythology. He was said to be the creator of the Earth, and struck fear into the hearts of gods and humans alike.

Odin had many adventures riding his fantastic white eight-legged horse, Sleipnir.

▼ **Stories tell how Sleipnir could gallop over land, sea and air.**

▼ **The unicorn was a magical white, horse-like creature with a twisted horn on its forehead. Legends say that it could only be tamed by a maiden.**

Ancient civilizations prized and respected horses above all other animals. Horses became symbols of status and wealth and the mounts of kings and warriors. So, naturally, the gods had horses, too, and ancient myths are full of tales of supernatural horses and horse-like creatures. Often, these horses were unruly and hard to control. Sometimes, they took on strange and terrifying forms.

Horses in war

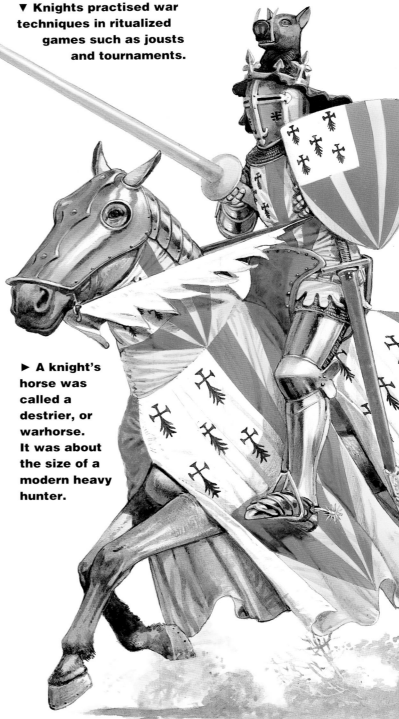

▼ Knights practised war techniques in ritualized games such as jousts and tournaments.

Imagine a cold grey morning, 5,000 years ago. Two desert tribes are lined up for battle, face to face, armed only with spears and axes. Suddenly, over the hill sweep the first horse-drawn chariots, carrying archers and warriors hurling spears. What a deadly surprise they must have been! The mobility horses gave to people changed the way of war forever and helped to shape history.

Armed riders have played a crucial part in warfare for centuries. It was only in World War I (1914-18) that tanks and powerful weaponry took horses out of the firing line.

► A knight's horse was called a destrier, or warhorse. It was about the size of a modern heavy hunter.

Call the cavalry!

In the Middle Ages, knights and horses wore armour in battle.

◄ Sumerian infantry and charioteers driving prisoners before them, from the Standard of Ur, *circa* 2,500 BC.

Although the armour helped to protect them, it also slowed the horses down. By the 1700s, fast-mounted soldiers called cavalry, armed with only swords or guns, became an army's main fighting force.

Bucephalus

The greatest cavalry leader of ancient times was the Macedonian king Alexander the Great, whose armies conquered half the known world. Alexander tamed the beautiful black horse Bucephalus, which no one else dared to ride. When Bucephalus died, Alexander built a city in its honour.

◄ Alexander on Bucephalus

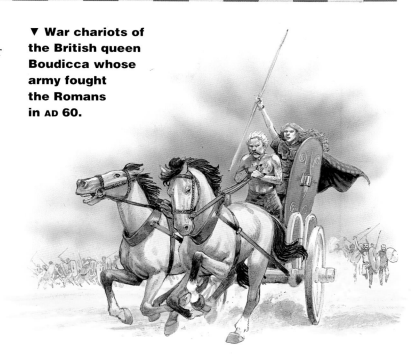

▼ War chariots of the British queen Boudicca whose army fought the Romans in AD 60.

Civil War

During the American Civil War (1861–65), both sides – the northern troops and the Confederates – had cavalry in their armies. Cavalry also carried messages between camps and scouted enemy positions.

▼ Approximately 375,000 horses were killed during World War I.

▲ General Ulysses S. Grant and his cavalry officers.

World War I

During World War I, tough and hardy horse breeds such as the Australian Waler were used as officers' mounts and for hauling artillery and ambulances.

Going places

For thousands of years before the days of cars, lorries, buses and trains, transport meant horses. Whether leading a packhorse, riding, or driving a carriage, anyone or anything going places went by horse power.

Fashion parades

In Europe, riding or leading a packhorse was often the best way to get around right up until the early 1600s. Gradually, roads and carriage design improved leading to the heyday of horse transport from the late 1600s to mid-1800s. Carriages soon became a status symbol and outings in the park were a chance for the rich to impress onlookers with their elegant, eye-catching turnouts. The high-stepping Hackney in Britain and the spirited American Morgan were two fashionable horse breeds much in demand for pleasure driving. Today, carriage driving competitions are held all over the world, keeping alive skills from the past.

Changing times

The building of the railways saw the end of the stagecoach era. But for shorter riding trips it wasn't until the early 1900s that the motor car finally replaced horse-drawn transport.

Phaeton carriage

Hansom cab

Hobby-horse

Hack

▲ In the Middle Ages, nobles and kings prided themselves on their magnificent Spanish and Arab horses.

Early people probably rode horses to hunt, but in ancient civilizations horses were mostly used as beasts of burden, harnessed to carts or war chariots. Riding was a sign of rank and nobility. It only became part of everyday life during the Middle Ages after saddlery was developed.

▲ Stagecoaches drawn by teams of fast, fit horses transformed communications and made long-distance travel possible for everyone.

Harness breeds

Horses used for pulling are called draught horses. Heavy draught refers to the biggest and strongest animals required for haulage work. Light draught horses are faster types with good endurance used for transport and drawing carriages.

Dray

Horse-drawn trolley bus

Pulling power

Until the Middle Ages, carts and ploughs were mainly pulled by oxen. Then, people in Europe discovered the breathtaking pulling power and intelligence of heavy horses, and for hundreds of years these placid, solid servants helped to plough the land, turn the mills and haul farm and factory wagons.

▼ Round and round in a tight circle – turning the millstones was a boring and exhausting task.

Horsepower
The word 'horsepower' is a modern-day reminder of the heavy horse's contribution to our world. Horsepower is a unit which is used to measure machine power (1 metric horsepower = 746 watts). How else could the salesmen of the new-fangled industrial machines describe them to customers who, like generations before them, had used horses for every imaginable job that needed doing!

Daily grind
Donkeys, mules and horses have been used to turn millstones to grind corn into flour since ancient times. Later, horse-wheels or 'gins' provided the power to keep early factory machines and furnaces running.

▲ The harness is a complicated arrangement of straps and buckles worn by draught horses. It enables the horse to pull its load and the driver to stay in control.

The progress made possible by the work of heavy horses helped to lay the foundations for the Industrial Revolution of the 1800s. Horse power was used to work machines and carry newly manufactured goods to ships for export. However, once steam engines were invented, the use of the heavy horse declined as its tasks were taken over by machinery.

Horse brasses

Ploughmen, carters and brewers have always proudly decorated their horses' harnesses with beautiful ornamental brasses. Originally, these were used as lucky charms and were thought to ward off evil.

▲ Each brass had a meaning. For example, the Sun meant good fortune.

On the land

A team of horses was as essential to the farmer of the past as a tractor is today. From the 1500s, horses were an absolute necessity for every task on the farm, from ploughing and harrowing (smoothing off) the fields to grinding the corn and transporting it to market.

▲ Some farmers are once again using heavy horses, such as the Shires on this small farm in Yorkshire, England. Many breweries, too, still use horse-drawn drays for local deliveries.

▼ A draught horse pulling a barge along a canal could pull 30 tonnes in weight.

Transport in tow

Until the railways arrived, the dependable barge horse kept the Industrial Revolution on the move. Canals became a cheap and reliable way to move raw materials such as coal, grain and cotton, to factories and manufactured goods to the cities and towns which needed them.

HORSES TODAY

You might think that cars, trains and tractors leave very little need for horses in today's world. It's true that nowadays only a small number of horses are bred for the traditional jobs they have done. However, although we may not depend on horses like our ancestors did, they are still very much part of our lives, if in different ways. Today, we have the chance simply to enjoy horses and ponies, to love being with

▲ Racing over huge steeplechase fences tests stamina as well as speed.

them, and to have fun riding them and developing their talents by training them for all kinds of sports.

▼ Polo is said to be the oldest and fastest team game in the world. It was invented by the Chinese over 1,500 years ago.

► In flat racing, jockeys use short stirrups to redistribute their weight and to help the horses gallop at their best.

On the beat

In cities as far apart as London, New York, Tokyo and Sydney, police horses can be seen patrolling the streets.

▼ **New York policewoman and her horse.**

These unflappable, superbly-trained horses give their riders a high viewpoint and the ability to move quickly in any direction – perfect for crowd control. Just a few of a police horse's other tasks include traffic duty, searching for missing people in a crowd or simply hoofing the beat.

Working horses

In many countries, donkeys, mules and horses still carry on their traditional roles of providing transport and a livelihood for their owners, as they have done for thousands of years.

All around the world, horses can still be found helping with tasks where machines cannot match their unique talents – from pulling tourist carriages in cities to rounding up cattle on a ranch or leading a big parade.

Cowboy horses

In cattle countries, cowhands have special names and ride special horses. North American cowboys usually ride a Quarter Horse, named after its amazing speed in a quarter-mile race. Mexican vaqueros work on fiery mustangs, while Argentinian gauchos ride the Criollo. Australian stockmen mostly use Walers – hardy horses bred by early settlers.

Donkey work

Sure-footed on the steepest mountainside and tough enough to keep going all day, donkeys and mules still work hard earning their living in countries such as Greece, Spain and Morocco.

◀ **This Moroccan donkey will carry its owner and several baskets of produce to market and back.**

▼ **The gaucho's lightning-quick horse works almost on instinct, picking out a calf from the herd. Once the calf is lassooed, the horse stops dead and throws its weight against the rope to hold it still.**

▼ **In many snowy north European countries, sturdy ponies pull sleighs carrying passengers, fuel or food.**

51

The entertainers

Horses are natural entertainers. Even an old pony turned loose in a field will show off with a kick and buck to a passing audience, and a star performer of the circus ring or sporting arena certainly knows it's special every time the crowd bursts into applause. Horses have topped the bill ever since the days of the spectacular chariot races in Ancient Rome. Today, their grace, strength and skill can still make us gasp whenever they step into the spotlight.

▼ The drum horse of Britain's Household Cavalry carries a huge pair of solid silver drums. The drummer steers by reins attached to the stirrups, but the horse never puts a foot wrong.

Ride 'em cowboy!

Rodeos began in the late 1800s in the cattle lands of North America. Today, professional cowboys keep traditional rodeo skills alive.

Circus horses

Animals are used less in circuses now but once the flowing manes and tails of the swirling Liberty horses were among the most breathtaking sights of the Big Top.

► *The Circus*, by Georges Seurat, 1891.

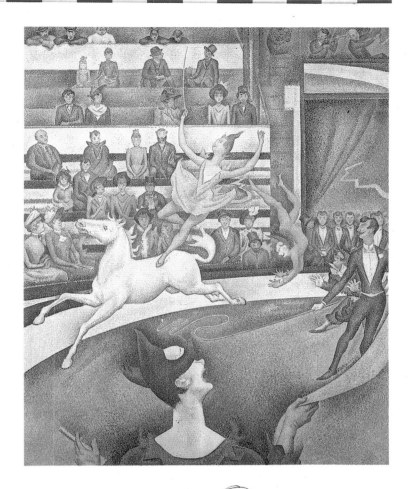

Pure poetry

The white horses of Vienna's Spanish Riding School are famous all over the world. The school is the oldest of several riding academies founded in the 1500s. It uses only Spanish horses, which for 400 years have been bred at Lipizza. Lipizzaner horses and riders take many years to train. Only the most gifted become the top haute école (high school) performers.

▲ Today's big rodeos have been called the greatest outdoor shows on Earth. Events include bronco riding, calf roping, steer wrestling and waggon racing.

A bronco rider has to try and stay on the back of a wildly bucking horse for at least 8 seconds – sometimes without a saddle!

53

Young riders

When you are with ponies, it doesn't matter how young you are or even if you have only just begun riding – there's always lots of fun to be had! A riding holiday, helping out at the stables after a lesson or joining the Pony Club (a worldwide organization for young riders) are great ways to learn more about riding and pony care. And when you're feeling brave, there's the excitement of your very first show.

At a show

There's something for everyone at a show. Horses and ponies that are especially handsome and obedient can take part in ridden showing classes ('under saddle') according to their type. Youngsters or pure-bred ponies can be shown off on a lead-rein (called 'in-hand'). In equitation classes that judge a rider's ability, ordinary four-legged friends can be winners, too!

◄ **Even the tiniest rider on a lead-rein pony can have a go at a gym-khana.**

Clear round

If you and your pony enjoy jumping there's sure to be a class to enter at a local show. Beginner riders can try the smaller jumps in the Minimus ring, where each

▲ **Jumping a natural fence at a Working Hunter show class.**

clear round wins a rosette. In other classes, ponies and riders of the same size or age and experience compete.

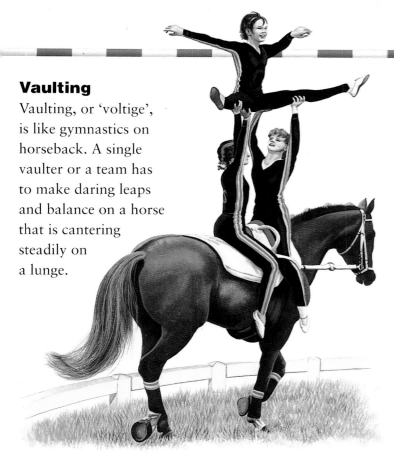

Vaulting

Vaulting, or 'voltige', is like gymnastics on horseback. A single vaulter or a team has to make daring leaps and balance on a horse that is cantering steadily on a lunge.

Perhaps your dream is to become a top showjumping or dressage rider one day. It may seem a daunting task, but don't forget – all famous riders started out by taking their pony to local shows and gymkhanas.

Disabled riding

All over the world, riding-for-the-disabled groups help people who would like to ride a pony to give it a try. Through RDA groups, riders can take riding lessons and participate in local shows, gymkhanas and even international competitions.

Ready, steady, go!

Gymkhana games are like some of the races at a school sports day. The only difference if that the contestants are on horseback. Games include flag races, sack races, apple bobbing and bending (racing in and out of a line of poles).

▼ Races at a gymkhana are fast and furious.

International sport

Today's competition horses are bred to be the very best at their particular sport – to gallop faster, jump higher or move with more grace and power than their rivals. Equestrian sports are different from any other sports. Not only must the horse be talented and fit, its rider must be too. A winning partnership means years of hard work and training, and to reach the top takes special teamwork.

Harness racing

Harness racing is popular in the United States and Russia, where breeds, such as the American Standardbred and the Orlov Trotter, have been developed especially for the sport.

▼ Some harness races are for pacing horses, which trot using the pair of legs on the same side rather than those diagonally opposite.

▼ The cross-country course at a three-day event usually provides plenty of thrills and spills.

Eventing

Eventing, or horse trials, is an all-round test of a horse and rider's fitness and skill. The competition has three phases – dressage, cross-country and showjumping. At the highest level, it takes place over three days.

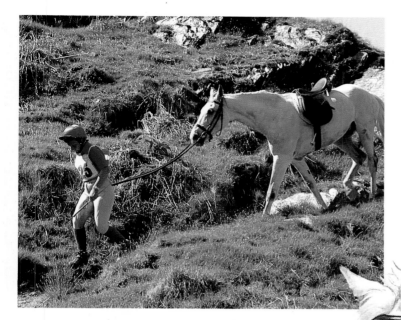

Showjumping

Showjumping has the same basic rules for a novice class at a local show and an international championship. The horse and rider must jump a course of coloured fences without picking up any faults from knocking one over or refusing. Riders with equal faults go again in a 'jump off', which may be timed, to decide the winner.

Dressage

'Dressage' means training. It aims to show the horse and rider in perfect harmony. Each pair performs a test of set exercises which are judged and awarded marks out of ten.

▲ Endurance races can cover up to 150 km in one or two days, often over difficult ground. Riders sometimes dismount during a race to rest their horses, which must pass strict checks by a vet.

Most event horses are Thoroughbreds, which have the combination of speed, boldness, stamina, good movement and big jump needed for this tough sport. Showjumpers need power and agility, while dressage horses must be supple and balanced with lovely paces.

Horse breeds

T oday, there are over 200 recognized breeds of horses and ponies. Breeds are groups of horses which have been bred to obtain particular features, such as colour, height, action and conformation. All these features are clearly defined, often by a breed society which keeps a special list, or a Stud Book of horses belonging to that breed.

Coloured horses

Certain colours of horse and pony are recognized as breeds in the United States, although in the rest of the word they are considered to be types (see below left).

NAME	HEIGHT	COLOUR
1 Appaloosa	14 – 15.2 hh	Spots unique to each horse; basic patterns include blanket, marble, leopard and snowflake
2 Palomino	varies	Golden with light mane and tail
3 Pinto	14-15.2 hh	Irregular patches of white and black or brown

Horse types

As well as breeds, there are also types. Instead of belonging to a breed with a Stud Book or pedigree, a type is produced by crossing other breeds to get a horse or pony suited to a particular purpose. The best known include the cob, hack, hunter, polo pony and riding pony. Most polo ponies are crosses between small Thoroughbreds and other breeds, such as the Argentinian Criollo. Despite usually being over 14.2 hh, they are always called ponies.

Riding ponies are suitable for young riders. They are usually cross-bred from Thoroughbreds or Arabs and native ponies.

◀ Riding pony

Ponies

All horses under 14.2 hh are called ponies. Pony breeds are strong and hardy with short-striding paces. Most ponies are quick-witted and full of character.

NAME	HEIGHT	COLOUR
4 Exmoor	11.2-12.2 hh	Bay, brown, dun
5 Welsh	Up to 13.2 hh	Any solid colour
6 Highland	12.2-14.2 hh	Usually grey, dun, brown or black; some-times bay or liver chestnut
7 Dales	13.2-14.2 hh	Mainly black or brown
8 New Forest	12-14 hh	Any solid colour
9 Connemara	13-14.2 hh	Mainly grey; also bay, brown, black or dun
10 Fjord	13-14.2 hh	Pale dun
11 Fell	13-14 hh	Bay, brown, black or grey
12 Dartmoor	Up to 12.2 hh	Any solid colour
13 Haflinger	13-14.2 hh	Palomino or chestnut with blond mane and tail
14 Shetland	Up to 42 in	Any colour
15 Riding pony	Up to 14.2 hh	Any colour

Little horses

A few pony breeds have features usually seen in horses rather than ponies but at a much smaller scale.

NAME	HEIGHT	COLOUR
16 Icelandic	12-14 hh	Any colour
17 Falabella	Up to 34 in	Any colour
18 Caspian	10-12.1 hh	Bay, chestnut or grey

Sports horses

Sports horses are either hot bloods or warm bloods. Arabs and Thoroughbreds are hot bloods. Warm-blood breeds come from crossing hot bloods and warm bloods.

NAME	HEIGHT	COLOUR
24 Arab	14-15 hh	Grey, bay, chestnut or black
25 Lipizzaner	15-16.1 hh	Usually grey, sometimes bay
26 Thoroughbred	14.2-17 hh	Most solid colours
27 Cleveland Bay	16-16.2 hh	Bay or brown
28 Barb	14-15 hh	Bay, brown, black, chestnut or grey
29 Andalucian	15.1-15.3 hh	Usually grey, also bay, black, chestnut or roan
30 Hackney	14-15.3 hh (horse) Under 14 hh (pony)	Bay, brown, chestnut, black
31 Selle Français	15-17 hh	Mostly chestnut, bay or brown
32 Waler	14.2-16 hh	Any solid colour
33 Quarter Horse	14.1-16 hh	Most colours
34 Akhal-Teke	14.2-15.2 hh	Bay, grey, black or dun with metallic sheen
35 Saddlebred	15-16 hh	Bay, black, grey or chestnut
36 Morgan	14-15.2 hh	Bay, black or chestnut
37 Standardbred	14-16.1 hh	Bay, brown, black or chestnut
38 Trakehner	16-16.2 hh	Any solid colour

Heavy horses

Today, most heavy horses are used for displays and shows rather than as work-horses.

NAME	HEIGHT	COLOUR
19 Shire	16-18 hh	Bay, black, brown, chestnut or grey
20 Suffolk Punch	15.3-16.1 hh	Always chestnut
21 Ardennais	15-16 hh	Mostly bay or roan
22 Clydesdale	16-17 hh	Bay, brown or black with white legs and face
23 Percheron	14.3-16 hh (Postier) or 16-17.3 hh	Usually grey, also black and roan

Glossary

action How a horse moves.

aged A horse over eight years old.

aid Signals a rider uses to communicate with a horse. Natural aids are the hands, seat, legs and voice. Artificial aids include whips, spurs and **martingales**.

bars 1) The parts of the gums at the sides of the mouth where there are no teeth and where the **bit** lies. 2) Metal hooks which are part of the saddle tree from which the stirrup leathers hang.

bit The part of the bridle which goes in the horse's mouth to give the rider more control.

bone The measurement around a horse's leg taken just below the knee. The more bone, the more weight a horse can carry.

breastplate A strap that goes round the horse's neck and fastens to the front of the saddle and between the forelegs to the girth. It stops the saddle slipping backwards, especially when galloping.

bridle The combination of straps which fit around a pony's head and are used to control it for riding.

brood mare **Mare** kept just for breeding.

brushing A kind of bad **action**, where the lower legs move so closely that they strike into each other.

cast When a horse lies down and is unable to get up.

chaff Straw, or a mixture of hay and straw, chopped into short lengths and added to the feed to provide more fibre.

MARE AND FOAL

clear round Completing a course of jumps without any penalties.

clip 1) Shearing off the winter coat to stop a horse from sweating too much when worked. 2) Part of a horseshoe that turns over the edge of the foot to help keep the shoe in place.

colic Horsey stomachache, often caused by bad feeding.

colt A young male horse under three years of age.

conformation The shape of a horse, or the way it is put together.

crupper A broad strap that is fixed to the back of the saddle going round the pony's tail, to stop the saddle from slipping back too far.

dam The mother of a foal.

dished face A face that has a concave profile, as in an Arab horse.

dishing A poor action, where the front feet are thrown out to the sides.

double bridle A bridle with two bits; used by highly-trained horses for dressage and showing.

dressage An elegant equestrian sport where horses are trained to be very obedient to their riders and perform a set of special movements.

eggbutt A T-shaped joint between the mouthpiece and rings of a bit, which stop the lips being pinched.

ergot Hard lump that can be felt at the back of the fetlock joint.

feather Long hair growing on the lower legs, especially in heavy breeds like the Shire or Clydesdale.

filly A young female horse under three years of age.

flehmen An odd, lip-curling expression made by horses and ponies when they smell or taste something interesting, or by a **stallion** interested in a **mare**.

BRIDLE
Headpiece
Browband
Reins
Throatlash
Cheekpiece
Noseband
Bit

foal A baby horse.

forehand The half of the horse in front of the saddle (*see* **hindquarters**)

forelock Section of mane that falls forward between the ears.

frog Rubbery V-shaped structure in the centre of the sole, under the hoof.

gall A sore around the belly caused by a girth that is dirty or too tight.

gamgee Cotton wool lined with gauze, used as padding under leg bandages.

gelding A castrated male horse.

gestation The length of time a foal is in the womb before being born. In horses, this is 11 months.

girth A broad strap place around the pony's belly to keep the saddle on.

going The condition of the ground for riding on – wet ground is called soft going and very dry ground is hard going.

green A young, inexperienced horse.

gymkhana A small show with games and races for ponies and their riders.

hackamore A type of bridle that does not use a **bit**.

halter A simple piece of headgear, often made of rope, for leading and tying up.

hand Unit of measurement of a horse's height. One hand equals approximately 10 cm (4 in).

headcollar Headgear made up of a noseband, headpiece and throatlash.

hindquarters The half of the body behind the saddle area (*see* **forehand**).

hogged mane When the mane is shaved off. Hogging is done to improve the appearance of horses with short, thick necks and coarse manes.

keepers The small leather loops used to hold the spare ends of the **bridle** straps neatly in place.

knee rolls Pads at the front of the saddle flaps which help keep the rider's legs in the correct position.

laminitis A painful disease that makes a pony's feet very tender – usually caused by over-eating.

leading leg The foreleg that stretches farthest forwards in canter.

loading Putting a horse or pony into a horsebox or trailer.

loose box An individual stable where a horse is kept and can be left loose.

lunge A long rein that is attached to a special headcollar called a lungeing cavesson. The trainer sends the horse around in a circle, using a lungeing whip to keep it going forwards.

manège An enclosed outdoor riding arena that usually has a surface that is good in all weathers.

manger A trough in a stable used for a horse's feed.

mare An adult female horse.

martingale Neckstrap attached between the forelegs to the **girth** and also the **reins** or noseband to give the rider extra control.

nappy Term used to describe a stubborn horse that won't go forwards, or hangs back towards its stable or friends.

near side The lefthand side of a horse (*see* **off side**).

HEADCOLLAR

neckstrap A strap around a pony's neck that a beginner rider can hold on to for safety. Also part of a **martingale** or **breastplate**.

New Zealand rug A tough rug for using outdoors in winter.

novice A beginner rider or inexperienced horse.

numnah A cotton or fleecy shaped pad used under the saddle to absorb sweat and ease pressure.

off side The righthand side of a horse (*see* **near side**).

over-reaching When a hind hoof hits the heel of a foreleg, causing injury.

pastern The area of the leg between the hoof and the fetlock.

Pelham Type of **bit** used with two **reins** and a curb chain; stronger than a **snaffle**.

picking out Cleaning out the hooves.

points 1) Parts of a horse. 2) The extremities of a horse, such as the muzzle, tips of the ears and lower legs, which are sometimes of a darker colour than the rest of the body.

pulling a mane/tail Taking out hairs, a few at a time, to neaten the mane or tail.

rein 1) The long straps attached to the **bit** used by the rider to control the pony 2) The direction a rider is going around an arena – being either on the left rein or the right rein.

roller A wide strap used around the belly to keep a rug in place.

Roman nose A convex profile, most often seen in heavy horses.

running up the stirrups Pushing the stirrup iron up the back of the leathers and threading the leathers through the iron to keep the stirrups tidy and safe when a pony is tacked up but not about to be ridden.

schooling Training a horse.

shying A sudden movement sideways after taking fright.

sire The father of a **foal**.

skipping out A speedy muck-out during the day using a basket 'skip' to collect the droppings.

snaffle Largest family of **bits**, with one ring either side of the mouthpiece.

sound A healthy horse that has no breathing or lameness problems.

RUGS

Day rug

Night rug

Horse blanket

surcingle A narrow strap used around the belly to fasten a rug, or over the saddle for extra security when galloping and jumping.

tack All the items of saddlery used for riding.

tacking up Putting on the **tack**.

tendons Tough tissue that connects muscles to bones. In horses, the main tendons run down the back of the cannon bones in the legs.

transition Changing from one pace to another.

tree The frame around which a saddle is built.

turning out Letting a pony loose into a field.

turn-out The appearance of a horse and rider.

vice A bad or nervous habit. Stable vices often start because a horse is bored. These include weaving, where the horse sways to and fro, crib-biting and wind-sucking, where it arches its neck and sucks in air. Vices shown out riding including rearing, napping (*see* **nappy**) and bucking.

wind A horse's breathing.

withers The top of the shoulder blade, which forms a bony ridge at the base of the neck. Horses and ponies are measured from the ground to the highest point of the withers.

yearling A one-year-old horse.

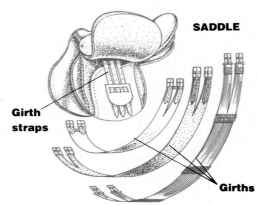

SADDLE

Girth straps

Girths

Index

Acknowledgements

The publishers would like to thank the following illustrators for their contribution to this book:

John Butler 6-7; **Peter Dennis** (Linda Rogers Associates) 38-43, 44-45*b*, 48-49, 52-53; **Angelika Elsbach** 30*bl*; **Lindsay Graham** (Linden Artists) 10-11, 22*bl*, 23, 32-33, 36-37, 56-57; **Ian Jackson** 8-9, 14-15, 34*l*, 35*tl*, 50-51, 54-55; **Eddy Krähenbühl** 16-17; **Ruth Lindsay** 17*r*, 21*b*, 27*br*, 30*c*, 34-35*bc*, 35*br*; **Nicki Palin** 18-19, 26-31, 44-45*b*; **Eric Robson** (Garden Studios) 4-5, 24-25; **Eric Rowe** (Linden Artists) 12-13; **Richard Ward** 5*r*, 6*bl*, 19*tr*, 20*bl*, 22*tr*, 27*c*, 30*t*, 32*tl*, 33*br*, 37*t*; **Wendy Webb** 20*tl* & *br*, 21*t*; **Steve Weston** (Linden Artists) 11*r*; **Andrew Wheatcroft** (Virgil Pomfret Agency) 58-59 **Dan Wright** 46-47

Woodcuts by Peter Cornwell
Border by Julian Baker

The publishers would also like to thank the following for supplying photographs for this book:

Page 11 Robert Harding Picture Library
14 The Granger Collection, New York
24 ZEFA
36 Robert Harding Picture Library
39 & 42 Michael Holford
43 Bridgeman Art Library/Library of Congress
45 Bibliothèque Nationale
48 Kit Houghton
51 ZEFA/Damm
54 Robert Harding Picture Library
55 & 57 Kit Houghton